Julia Bittner

# *A beautiful day in September*

L·E·P
MOTIVATION

Original edition, 1st edition, 2024
Date of first publication: 01.09.2024

All rights reserved. Reproduction in whole or in part, in any form (electronic data processing, photocopying or other processes), duplication and distribution of copies only with the written permission of the author.

All photographs used in this book are the intellectual property of Julia Bittner. Passing on and reproduction of the photographic products of this publication is prohibited.

Cover design: Julia Bittner
Cover illustration: Julia Bittner
Image rights: Julia Bittner

Printed in Germany
978-3-911030-51-9

1. Hello September — 9

2. Josie — 17

3. Love in September — 23

4. John — 31

5. The day of change — 41

6. You are gone — 55

7. Letters to you — 65

8. Trance — 83

9. Reconsideration — 91

10. Visions of the future — 99

11. Our heaven — 111

12. Tomorrow — 121

Epilogue

## 1 Hello September

Hello world. Hello September. A new month begins! The sun is shining, I've slept well, and the first day of September can begin.

Do you know the feeling you get when everything seems to be fine on certain days, your problems are far away and things couldn't be better for you? Today, September 1st of this year, was just such a day for me.

I was walking along the small park at the end of our street and caught the first rays of sunshine. The richly leafed entrance gate, which was interspersed with rose tendrils, beamed at me in yellow, red and pink.

The elegant rose plants stretched out their most beautiful blossoms towards me, and I passed through the gate with ease to get to the fairground.

So that I could take the right path, I walked down a fork at the end of the park on the left.

The square was quite centrally located, so many paths led to it. But the walk through the romantic park had always been my favorite.

It was a beautiful, sunny day, so I was only wearing a denim blue sweater and a black skater skirt. I loved casual clothes that still had a feminine touch. For me, things had to be practical but chic at the same time. My matching sneakers in sky blue rounded off my outfit.

They shone brightly against the blue September sky, and it was clear to me that this was a picture-perfect day in September.

I wore my long, curly black hair loose, but hid most of it under a wine-red cap. My sweater was embroidered with a glittering book.
I've loved reading a lot since I was a child, so I wanted to express my affinity for books through my clothes.
It wasn't easy for me to communicate with others in a harmonious way, so I loved clothes that signaled my interests to the other person. That way, everyone knew right away without me having to talk much.
That was my way of communicating with others. It kept me from putting my foot in my mouth or offending other people - because I had a real talent for that!

Sometimes I could be very moody and quickly get on other people's nerves with my manner.
I wasn't the most patient person, except when I was reading books and could then immerse myself in my own world.
Reading made me forget everyday life and took me into an existence that was often hidden from me in "real" life.
Stories of adventurers, courageous women who stood up to injustice, dramatic romance novels or dreamy fairy tales set in completely different universes immediately captivated

me. I loved these stories so much because my life was anything but a fairy tale.

There was only boredom here, and my emotional outbursts were limited to acquiring bargains, which I got when I didn't have to pay full price for a book.
No glitter and certainly no action. I led a very "normal" life, as most of my relatives liked to describe it. I wasn't proud of it, but what could I do?

As I mentioned before, I loved clothes that reflected my character. I chose expressive clothes because I had a lot to say in a world that didn't let me have my say.

My clothes reflected what I liked, but not necessarily that I didn't care much for other people.
My behavior towards others was often harsh. My style of dress, on the other hand, often seemed delicate, even playful at times. One could assume that I wanted to deceive people visually so that they would like me despite my clumsy manner.
I could be loud, quick-tempered and cold towards other people. I had often put one or two people off with this behavior.

But today was not the time to let this side of me out - because today was the perfect day in September!

---

The ninth month of the year had always been my favorite time of year because it had everything I loved so much. The harbingers of autumn were already showing as the leaves on some of the trees were starting to change color.
At the same time, a little bit of summer could still be seen in September, for example when the last sunflowers bloomed or a small group of bees circled the largest and most colorful flowers.
Nature gradually transformed the green landscape into a sea of red, yellow and orange hues and the sky this month was also very special for me, as it made the clouds glow in a magical, warm light.
I walked almost carefree through the streets of my hometown, and at that time could not have guessed what misfortune would befall me in my young life.

---

September ushered in the cozy autumn days and when the first leaves fell from the trees, I was completely in fall mode.

When I arrived at the fairground, it was already full. As it quickly became too crowded for me, I ran up a hill that was right next to the fairground. I ran up it without taking a break, quickly passing the small field of sunflowers, which were already fading at this time of year, and was delighted when I finally reached the top.

From here I could see all the hustle and bustle, including the shining eyes of children, and hear the joyful laughter. It was also the highest point in my hometown - and if you ask me, the most beautiful spot with the best view!
It was a great sight to see here. And the best thing about it: I was almost always alone up here. Nobody dared to climb the mountain because the ascent was very steep and exhausting.

As I watched the many happy children and young people from the mountain and heard the cheerful sounds, I knew: it's September, the best month of the year and I was right in the middle of it!

## 2 Josie

I had always been a very lively child and can still remember how my mother was often called to the principal of my school - because I had so much energy that I disrupted the lessons or simply couldn't concentrate on the tasks at hand.

My mother always made it very clear to the principal that this was simply my nature: *"Josephine is not a rebellious child. You just need to adjust better to her sensitivities and encourage her God-given talents more!"*.
My mother defended me every time, and did so very vehemently in a very insistent - almost theatrical - tone of voice. I think she even took a little pleasure in the fact that I stood out from the crowd.

Under no circumstances would she have accepted anyone mistreating or criticizing her child. My mother was a strong woman and I always admired that about her.
Even as a child, she encouraged me to be myself and not let myself be bent. As a result, I was able to develop according to my talents and mature into an extraordinary person, just like my mother.
She encouraged me in everything I wanted to try. I think this was because she hadn't enjoyed much freedom herself in her childhood.

She obviously wanted to do things differently with me - and she succeeded quite well!

---

I had always been a very passionate person. You could see this in the way I behaved in private and in the way I looked. My hair could never be tamed because I had long, curly black hair. The curls made it look like I had a lot more hair than was actually the case.
It took me hours to style or blow-dry it. As a child, I often hated this peculiarity of my hair and I wanted straight hair. Looking back, I don't think any other hair would have suited me and my temperament better than these wild curls.

---

My birthday, at the end of September, was always celebrated in style. I was loved by all family members and had a really nice childhood.
Although my relatives led a relatively quiet, inconspicuous life, I liked them very much.
Unfortunately, due to my very lively nature, I had very few friends and found it difficult to make new ones. My temperament quickly became too much for many people.

I was interested in artistic things, enjoyed reading, and spent hours thinking about life and its meaning.

The counterbalance to these quiet activities was practical things. Everything that came into my head had to be put into practice as soon as an idea came to me. I was also very volatile.
Although I was a very loud child, there were also many moments when I retreated into my own world to be alone with myself.

I needed this separation so that I could collect myself and be myself again. That is probably also the reason why so few people noticed me, and I believed at the time that it would stay that way forever.

---

I actually only had two good friends in my childhood. Unfortunately, they both moved away before I turned 14. Establishing and maintaining contact with other, new people was never particularly easy for me.
Although I seemed very confident on the outside, I was hardly ever confident on the inside. I felt alone because nobody was like me. I also always had an ideal idea of perfect friends or the perfect partner.

Even though I seemed confident and strong, I wanted nothing more than to have one person in my life who understood me and was like me.

I believed that my dream would never come true and that I would have to stay alone forever. But my wish did come true - years later on a beautiful day in September...

## 3 Love in September

My life was perfect every day in September. I loved romping through the colorful leaves that the trees had already shed. Life was good. In the afternoon, I made my way to our local library before heading home with my latest 'achievements'.

My favorite author, Jen Johnson, had just recently published her latest book titled "*The Skyway*".
I read this masterpiece completely in two days. One passage in the book particularly touched me. The passage read as follows:

*"And if we die tomorrow, can we say that we have done everything in our power? The vultures are circling above us.*

*I can hear them making fun of us. Mocking the stupidity that rules us. That holds us captive. We can't find a way out.*

*We are condemned to look into the abyss. But do we want to see it? Or will we only be left with the realization at the end of our days that we haven't done enough?"*

Sometimes time moves so fast that we hope we can stop it now and again. But it runs relentlessly against us.

Like a treadmill that will never stop. It is up to us to seize opportunities and keep up with the pace of the treadmill. If we jump off, we drop out of life and the opportunities pass us by.

Keep up the pace.

Keep up.

Keep running.

The treadmill forces us to keep going, even when we are out of breath. As if there is an invisible force that controls our thoughts and actions. I, too, have often asked myself what will remain of us if we leave this world and opportunities remain unused.

---

The first orange leaf fell at my feet as I sat lost in thought on the park bench in front of the library. I felt the warm breeze of the fall wind and knew that today was not the day to be melancholy. I still had so much to do, and no one could take this day in September away from me.

---

My mood was getting better by the minute. Today is the middle of the month. I was up early and then slipped right into my sky blue sneakers to greet the new day.
As usual, I'm a little late, but I hurry to the park because I can't miss today's meeting.

It's Saturday and for once a year, something exciting happens in my hometown: the annual funfair begins.
I smell the aroma of fresh pastries and can hardly wait to get my hands on the sweet treats. I sprint through the park, past the Rose Gate again, and I arrive at the fairground faster than ever before. Crowds of people bustle around the rides and food stalls. It's a familiar sight for me.

I've decided that I'm going to have fun today, even without anyone by my side. I ride every attraction, visit all the food stalls and stuff myself with all kinds of sweets until I'm almost bursting. Sated, I sit down on the beach that stretches around the fairground.

It is an artificial sandy beach that has only recently been created. That's why the sand is as soft as absorbent cotton as I slide my exhausted feet into it.
The sun is just setting and makes the sky glow in the most beautiful colors.

I feel sad, all this comfort can't cheer me up. I can feel a tear running down my cheek. Now I know for sure: September can also make me think.

---

Today, on the last day of September, I sat in the library as usual and watched the hustle and bustle outside the building walls. I had noticed that I had never really taken in all the details of the stonework with my eyes.

Only now did I notice the small decorations, the beautifully draped stucco on the ceiling and the historic-looking entrance hall.
Everything seemed to be very old. The furniture made a very well-kept impression. All the corridors smelled of knowledge and history.

---

In the evening, I looked out of my bedroom window. The moon was shining in brightly and I think it must have been a full moon. Its light framed the leaves of the chestnut tree outside my window.

The incidence of light caused the leaves to cast a fascinating shadow on my desk. Winter would soon be upon us.

I ended this day like any other in September: I picked up a book, read it until my eyes closed, and woke up the next morning to a new month. Before I fell asleep, I looked at the beautiful moon again. Full moon phases are supposed to be very inspiring and challenging.

What would the world have in store for me? Would I be facing new challenges or enlightenment?

## 4 John

As lively and wild as I was, I rarely got involved with people who didn't understand this way of life. As a teenager, I looked after my own affairs for the most part. I was happy with myself and my personality and, as I mentioned, I hardly had any friends, but I wasn't dependent on anyone either. I loved my independence - until I met YOU.

The moment that changed my life from the ground up happened on a warm September day in our public library. The library had become my second home, and I had long since counted the many books among my true friends.
I had once again made myself comfortable on one of the old wooden chairs right by the entrance.
From here, I had a wonderful view of the whole room, which was lined with countless bookshelves. What's more, my favorite spot was right by the window, so I could see the trees, still full of leaves, which were slowly beginning to shed their foliage.
Like every day, I tried to soak up the knowledge of an entire book, as I was now very practiced at speed reading. Just as I was finishing the end of a chapter, a young man suddenly entered the room. I had never seen him before. But when he walked through the door, it was like being struck by lightning. I was transfixed by his gaze.

A pleasantly warm feeling ran through my body. I had never seen anyone so beautiful until that day. Everything about him was just right. He was tall, dark-haired and had ice-blue eyes. His gaze captivated me from the very first second.

When we first met, he was wearing simple jeans with a white shirt and a baseball jacket over it, but he could have worn any other outfit, because he was perfect for me.
He didn't look like someone who came from this town. I wondered if he had recently moved here or was just vacationing in this sleepy little town.

I had also never seen him in the library before - which led me to believe that he wasn't from this area, as I knew almost every member, because I was here every day.
I didn't realize at first that I had been staring at him for quite a while, as my mind kept wandering, and I became completely absorbed in his gaze.
I must have been inattentive for a very long moment, because suddenly our eyes crossed. Completely perplexed, I didn't really know what to do.
Could I withstand his gaze? Was it better to look away or stand firm? Nervousness now flowed through my body and I suddenly felt uncomfortable.

After what felt like an eternity, the sight of him brought me back to reality and our eyes consciously met as he looked over at me. Who were you and why were I so magically attracted to you?

---

This feeling was new to me. You looked at me as if you could see straight into my heart. I felt that I wanted you in my life. The sudden calm that spread through me was new for me. All of a sudden, my wild side had disappeared and I became very quiet.
I didn't want you to go away like the others. I didn't want to scare you. Looking at you gave me a wonderful feeling and I made every effort not to be harsh and dismissive this time. Your eyes revealed your innermost being to me and let me look straight into your soul. From that moment on, I knew that there could be no coincidences.
That day, I wore a polka-dotted black and white dress, white sneakers and spontaneously put on my best smile. Miraculously, this seemed to work, because you came towards me quickly. The closer you got, the more I recognized your beauty.
You had freckles and your complexion was slightly tanned, so it looked as if you had just come back from vacation.

Maybe I was right in my assumption and you were just passing through? Your jet-black hair framed your face because it was slightly longer than a short haircut, but still short enough so that it didn't fall into your face.

Your baseball jacket graced the lettering of another city - perhaps this was your home? While I was still staring at you, mesmerized, you asked me if I knew my way around this library and where the philosophy section was.

Your voice sounded like music to my ears. You smiled at me when you asked, and your posture told me that you were probably rather shy too.
Stuttering, I gave you directions. Although I was very eloquent, I forgot to speak at that moment. I blacked out and all the words disappeared at once. Unfortunately, I wasn't brave enough to walk you straight there - I could barely look at you, so how was I supposed to walk just a few steps with you?

I think you sensed it very clearly. You came closer and asked me if I could accompany you, and I agreed. You shook my hand and introduced yourself as John.
Due to my great interest in various literature, I knew that John means something like "God is gracious". And yes, God was gracious because he had sent you to me - I could

hardly believe my luck. We spent an exciting afternoon in the library. And although we didn't talk much and spent a lot of the time just looking at each other, I realized that this wasn't our last meeting.

---

You know those people who come into our lives and whose peculiarities stay with us forever? The way someone wears their hair, a distinctive eye color or the sound of their voice when they laugh? Details that we will never forget.

These memories stay in our hearts and in our memories forever, flickering even if we haven't seen a person for ages. John had that special quality. I would still recognize his eyes 50 years from now among thousands of people because they were so unique. His look, which seemed so familiar and mysterious to me every time we met - I would probably never get enough of him.

---

From that day on, we met almost every day at the place where we first met: the local library. I was overjoyed, because the more time I spent with you, the more intensely I felt how close we were.

The invisible bond between us grew stronger and stronger and seemed unshakable to me. Now I had everything I needed: my favorite person in my favorite place, could life get any better?

Hour after hour we got to know each other better, talked about God, the world, our views on life and discussed why there were people who didn't like books. We agreed that we were absolutely suspicious of these people.
We became a couple and spent a whole four years together. The years I spent with you were the four best years of my life so far. Before that, I had never met anyone who was more observant than you. You noticed the little things.

Every day, when you were on your way to me, you passed the little field of sunflowers on the mountain. As I once told you that these were my favorite flowers, you always brought me a blossom or a bunch.

---

Even on prom day, you were my date as a matter of course. When we were together, time stood still. Every time we met, it seemed like it was never any different. Like it was meant to be. I forgot everything I knew before you. You looked at me and suddenly there was only the here and now.

No one brought me the peace of mind that you gave me as soon as you were by my side. At the time, you said that my glittering red dress with a slit accentuated my skin and hair color particularly well.

Of course, I didn't believe a word you said at the time because I was young and full of insecurities. Despite everything, my prom was beautiful, and it was only because of you. You made me feel like a princess that night. I am very grateful to you for that.

---

You were always in a good mood, polite and - what I liked most about you - incredibly optimistic.
Nothing could shake you. I could lean on your strong shoulder and that was just perfect for four years.

Your favorite food was sushi, so we decided to take a sushi cooking course together after we moved in together. However, as we only had eyes for each other during the course, the subsequent test cooking at home ended with an upset stomach. That was pretty bad - but I knew I could get through anything with you.

At the time, I would never have guessed that our meeting wasn't all positive. How can you imagine something you're not prepared for?

# 5 The day of change

How can you explain something to others if you can't understand it yourself? When every thought of it tears your heart apart, and you fear drowning in memories?
I felt like a traveler who had lost sight of her light on the open sea and was now drifting aimlessly. It was dark around me. All the lights had gone out, and I was all alone.

The love that once filled my heart was gone. You feel like you're dying inside, while the rest of the world just keeps on living. How can that be possible?
Do you also know those days when everything goes wrong, and it seems as if all your problems come together on that very day? The universe seems to be working against you, and even the smallest spark of hope is nipped in the bud.

Today is just such a day.

But from the beginning.

I will try as best I can to describe the unbelievable. Even if I fear that the more I tell you about it, the more I will lose myself.

---

When you left this world, it was still a beautiful day in September for me. I didn't feel that you had quietly left this world. It was no wonder, as our strong bond was no longer as unbreakable as it used to be. We had cut it. We had parted ways, and our connection had simply been broken over the great physical distance.

I can only guess what happened to you on that dark day in September. We hadn't been in contact for six years. That's why it's difficult for me to understand what happened that night, because I perceived you as a different person than you have been for the last few years.

---

I found out from the newspaper that you must have been in a terrible car accident. You drove off the road in the pouring rain. You were probably driving too fast.
In this accident, you were thrown out of the car onto the rain-soaked road. You were still alive at the time - at least that's what the emergency services think.

You lay unconscious on the road. I can only imagine how terrible it must have been for you to lie there alone, in pain and full of fear. A driver who happened to be driving along this road only found you two hours after the accident.

The paramedics who arrived tried to look after you as best they could. In order to save your life, they initiated a number of resuscitation measures - to no avail.

I wish I could have been by your side at this time and been able to touch you or talk to you. It breaks my heart that your last hours ended so lonely. You deserved so much more than that. You had so many plans, but fate had a different plan for your life.

You died at the scene of the accident and were dead before you could be saved - they say. On September 16 at 3.45 pm, you left this world forever. One of the many tests your body underwent after the accident could not rule out alcohol abuse.

You and alcohol? The John I knew was obsessed with reading and certainly not into drinking. I wondered what kind of person you had become.

---

After I found out about your death and the circumstances, I looked for reasons for your change. Did I even know you anymore? I tried to remember you as you were when we first met.

You were the most loving and warm person I knew. You brightened my day and I think I made your life a lot better too. Like me, you had few friends, but we didn't need anyone once we were together.
The strong bond between us was always present and seemed unshakable. I had never felt so close to a person before. We looked in the same direction and would have given up everything for each other at any time.

---

Because I was so confused about your development over the last few years, I went looking for you on internet forums. I hadn't looked through your profile for a long time. I was afraid that it might hurt me too much if I saw your new, presumably happy life.

I didn't find anything at the beginning of my search. I could only find one profile that bore your name and already existed when we were still together. You had always placed little value on social media, so I wasn't surprised that you hadn't created any other accounts since we broke up.

So your old profile was still there - but the old John wasn't. Your new profile picture, uploaded three weeks before you died, shows a different John to the one I knew back then.

You've grown up, grown a beard and wear chic clothes. You didn't use to care about that. A pair of jeans and a T-shirt were always good enough for you. And that suited you best of all, I thought.

---

When we met in the library, I was just about to finish my A-levels and you were looking for a place at university.
In the end, you chose philosophy as your subject. It suited you well because you've always had a way with words and thought about the boldest things.

When you finally graduated from university, we were still together. I'll never forget how good you looked on graduation day. The black gown made your dark hair shine even brighter, and your blue eyes stood out.
It was an exciting day, although there had already been a crisis between us for a long time. After we broke up, you applied for a master's degree at a university far away from me.

I think you did that on purpose to get away from us and our dilemma. I can't even blame you, because I couldn't stand us and the constant arguments at that time either.

---

Some time has passed since then, and you seem to have moved in a different direction in the last six years. Maybe, no definitely, you have met new people. People who have influenced you differently than I did.
Oh John, WHAT happened? How did we become SO? How did YOU get to this point? A point of no return. Everything that made you was no longer there.

The John I knew was no longer there.

---

When I tell your story and speak the truth out loud, I feel that I still can't comprehend it. It's as if the world has to stop because you are no longer in it. But it doesn't. It keeps spinning as if nothing had happened.

What will your end have looked like? The moment you passed into the afterlife. What will you have thought or felt? Perhaps you weren't unconscious immediately and experienced everything consciously. I imagine your spirit, after it has left your body, floating high up in the sky.

It leaves the rain-covered clouds behind and flies into freedom. You fly as far as you can. Nothing saddens you anymore. This fate is accepted as naturally as the air we breathe.

But stop: YOU are no longer breathing. You also feel no fear of falling and ask no more questions. Your soul becomes very light, and you are free from fear, pain and doubt. What happened a moment ago on earth no longer concerns you. There is nothing but joy and bliss, just like on every beautiful day in September.

---

While your soul is long gone, your lifeless shell is discovered by the rescue workers. Some look at you with pity because they have sons and daughters your age and think you were far too young to die.

You had your whole life ahead of you. Now you will never experience what it feels like to get married, to have children, to celebrate - because you can hold a new employment contract in your hand - or to cry because loved ones have passed away.

You can no longer have all these experiences. You can no longer feel human emotions. I wonder what you are like on the other side. What role do you play in heaven? Where is your place there?
Is there really only your soul left in this place? A reflection of your human being with all your thoughts and feelings? Or are you simply living another version of your life on earth on the other side?

Can you remember what you were like here? Have your memories been extinguished? Do you remember what your human life was like here on earth?
Are you aware that you have died? Are you aware of how you died? And if so, are you sad that you can no longer participate in all our lives?

---

I imagine you looking down on us. I firmly believe that the souls of the deceased can visit all the places that they visited before they died and that are therefore known and familiar to them.
The energy of these places magically attracts these souls. Places with a particularly strong emotional connection are easier for the souls to find than places with which they do not have so many memories.

Have you visited our fairground? Or the library where our eyes met for the first time? Or maybe you had long forgotten me before you left us. Your memories of our good times have probably faded for a while, and you've built a new life with new people who now fill your memories.

---

According to your profile, you have a master's degree in finance and worked as a financial management consultant in a prestigious office until you passed away. When you and I were still together, we used to laugh our heads off at such consultants.

Mainly because many representatives of this profession are dogged and often take themselves and their job too seriously. We couldn't understand that at all. When we were together, there was nothing but fun, joy and in-depth conversations.

---

Did you really become one of these consultants? Did you also see your life as grim or did you work like crazy without really enjoying life?

You probably traded fun and lifetime for overtime and everyday stress. I can't imagine the John I knew, the old version of you, in this role at all. This thought gives me the creeps and a cold shiver runs down the back of my neck. If we had met by chance in the last few years, I think I would have thought I was seeing ghosts. You in a suit?
No, I couldn't believe it.

I just don't like the idea of it. The new John version perhaps liked the prestige and all the money that came with the job. Your profile picture shows me that you're still very good-looking. But instead of jeans and a T-shirt, you're really wearing a suit now.

When I look at your profile picture, I realize that I'm still talking about you as if you were here and part of my life. You are still alive in my mind. You have only uploaded a few pictures yourself, but some people have linked to you in other photos.

These pictures show a completely different John.
John at countless parties, at company dinners with bosses and colleagues - or John posing shirtless with a few women. I wonder if you've found someone who really suits you and your life. Someone who likes you as a person and your new life just as much. Do YOU fit into your new life?

Do you like it, or do you sometimes wish you had made a different decision and your life would have been different as a result? For my part, I haven't yet been able to find anyone who was anything like you.

No one has the special charisma, the smile that enchanted me every time, or even the slightest bit of emotional intelligence that you gave me every day. I can't find any information about your relationship status on your profile.

But the pictures with you and many different women tell me that you probably haven't found the one person for your life yet. So what is the logic behind YOU having to leave this world when you haven't yet experienced everything that life has to offer?

Death begins with our birth. We die a little more every day. The sand in our clock of life flows incessantly towards the end.

---

Like me, you also liked to write poetry. I can still vividly remember a poem you wrote me for my birthday in the last year of our relationship.

The title was simply: *"To Josie"*.
It ended with the words, *"... even the most beautiful flower fades after a while. But in me, our garden of love will flourish forever"*. When I remembered your words, I felt that my heart was already withering.

## 6 You are gone

Do you remember how I told you that September is my favorite month? Well, today, on this sunny day in September, is one of the saddest days for me.

A moment ago my world seemed to be in order, but now there is nothing left of it. I walked to the little park at the end of our street. As usual, I walked through the gate of the park, which was surrounded by rose bushes and lush, dark green hedges.
This park always had something magical about it for me, because it was romantic and dreamy at the same time. At the end of the park, there was a fork in the road leading in two directions. I was able to switch off here and felt safe. I often took the left-hand path because it led me to the fairground.

I used to spend my free time on this fairground not so long ago when I wasn't hanging out in the library. It had become my second favorite place. I loved the sounds of the rides, the smell of candy floss and almonds and, of course, the loud music that always put me in a carefree mood.
John loved this place too. He loved the fairground and always referred to it as our secret passageway.

Although it wasn't a passageway, just a simple path, the name made it a bit more mysterious.

---

We loved secrets and all things magical. Even in the early stages of getting to know each other, we confided everything without exception. I didn't find it difficult to trust John, and I think he felt the same way about me.

I think we would have made good detectives too. Because our interest in the unexplained and unsolved criminal cases was immense. Whenever I philosophized about how crazy some crimes were, John always said to me:
"*Josie, we'll set up a detective agency and investigate unsolved cases - we'll be really successful with that!*".
We had already found a suitable name for the detective agency: **Secret Service J&J - nothing goes undetected with us!**

OK, the name wasn't particularly imaginative, but it was enough to get us started. Of course, John knew as well as I did that we were still far too young to set up a company, but that didn't bother us.

The day would come when we could realize our project. Now I have to rephrase that sentence: Unfortunately, we will never be able to realize this project again. The new name is: **Secret Service J&J - with us, your secrets will remain undiscovered forever.**

---

Ever since we visited the fairground together for the very first time, it became our favorite place. We spent many hours at this joyful place, rode the colorful rides countless times, and then stuffed our bellies with candy until we felt sick.

Every day was beautiful with you. I never felt sad again when I went on the rides because you were there. I can still hear our hilarious laughter today when we rode the so-called "*Speed Tower*", where the wagon first slowly went all the way to the top and then suddenly and mercilessly plummeted downwards in a very short time.

Once again, if we couldn't wait to eat the treats at the fair, we did so before the ride on the *Speed Tower*. The sweet stuff we had eaten beforehand now reached the upper part of our bodies in no time at all and put so much pressure on our stomachs that we felt sick after the ride - and decided to take a break from riding for the rest of the day.

---

But today I didn't turn left to get to the fairground like I usually do; nor did I pass the relaxing oasis in the middle of the park, which was framed by magnificent trees.
No, today is the funeral of my former friend. The funeral of the one person who had always helped me in my youth. It's the funeral of the person who was my whole world back then.

John died on September 16, suddenly and without warning. We hadn't been in touch for years, but I held the memory of him in my heart to this day. These thoughts are still so full of joy and vivid moments, that I thought it was only yesterday.

----

I had just turned 18, John was two years older than me. He was also my first love and my hero. I liked him straight away. He was tall, dark-haired and had this energy in his eyes that drew me to him from everywhere. Not only that, but he had this aura that only a few people can call their own. This kind of aura can't be learned or bought for money. You either have it or you don't.

We shared everything back then: our fears, our dreams and planned big. We even moved in together after a short time because we were sure that our relationship would last forever.

Our apartment wasn't big, but it had everything we wanted. We didn't have enough money for more than a two-room apartment, but we didn't care because we wanted to spend every minute together anyway.

Back then, I thought life was endless. How wrong I was about that. We spent summer days together on the beach next to the fairground, wrapped ourselves in cozy blankets in winter, and had never spent a night apart since we first met.

Nothing could keep us apart - or so I thought. After a few years, however, John's behavior changed fundamentally. He had become selfish and cold-hearted. Loving conversations became brief small talk. There were no deep conversations or other emotional attention.

The magic between us had evaporated. We could no longer hold on to the mystery that had previously connected us, and so it slipped out of our hands. We let our happiness wither away until it finally died.

---

Our visits to the fairground became shorter, until we soon stopped going at all. Autumn had arrived, and yet I knew that there would be no next spring or summer in our relationship.
We had grown tired of each other and I felt as if this relationship had been caught in a snowstorm, and we were both buried under a thick, heavy blanket of snow. We both struggled to find our way out of the masses of snow. But unfortunately, we didn't succeed.

John's rescuing hand had already sunk into the snow and I could no longer grasp it. He had already been caught up in the emotional ice age that now prevailed between the two of us. In the end, we had to admit that the cold had got the upper hand. We became strangers to each other. So estranged that we simply gave up after a while.

---

Today - almost ten years later - I realize that nothing lasts forever. In a few years, no one will remember your existence, John. The fact that our lives will end at some point, that all the love, the times we laughed, cried or argued will be over, tears me apart.

Everything is so fleeting, I realize that now, on the day of your funeral. You were here just a moment ago and now you're gone. Just like that. You've changed sides. You decided to leave - without coming back.

But just like you, the memories of you will die. You will crumble to dust. Your deeds, feelings and how you shaped this world will all pass away. The next spring will certainly not come for you.

## 7 Letters to you

Today, the last day of September, is not a nice day. Everything is loud. I'm surrounded by people who are crying because of you. There's a loud buzzing in my head and I can't think straight. My eyes are burning because I've cried so much for you.
Life seems so fragile to me, and your funeral makes me feel more vulnerable than ever before. Your death was not logical. Nothing about it makes sense. The fact that we commemorate you on this day and that your parents had to plan your funeral is just as illogical to me as the fact that I will never see you again.
I can't explain it to myself, and it turned my world upside down. Everything I believed in was called into question with your death. It's pure chaos in my head.

---

I only know a fraction of the people attending your funeral. Your mother and father are crying in each other's arms. The look on their faces tells me that they can't believe what's happening. I can hardly believe it myself. As I am constantly plagued by mental and physical pain, which occurs so intermittently that I can hardly hold back my tears, I stay in the background.

I can see your sister walking past me. I always liked her a lot. She has the same beautiful, pitch-black hair and your ice-blue eyes. Despite the sad occasion, her eyes shine and when I look at her, I see you.
The moment our eyes meet, all I can think about is you. Your sister is so much like you that I think I can look into your soul and not hers in that one moment.

---

You are buried in a gray coffin that glistens slightly in the light. Your coffin has been laid out and placed at the end of the room. We haven't seen each other for a long time, but I recognize you immediately. It is your aura that immediately captivates me again.
All of a sudden, all the thoughts and experiences with you that I had suppressed until then come flooding back into my mind. I didn't want to open this box of memories, and now you're forcing me to. Is that fair?
I'll wait until your parents and your sister have left your coffin and there's enough space for me to step forward.
I would prefer to be alone with you.
I now stand with my back to the mourners, and it feels as if I can literally feel the stares of the others. I don't want everyone to see my grief.

I don't want everyone to see that I'm crying for you. As I approach your coffin, I feel my legs slowly threatening to break away.
I am now standing here, praying and hoping that I won't faint. The situation is completely overwhelming for me and my body.
I look at your face, at your soft features and the dark hair that frames your face evenly one last time. It seems as if you're just sleeping and will wake up any second.

I'm waiting for you to wake up and tell me that this was all just a bad joke - but you don't. Your hands are crossed on your chest. I dare to touch one of them.
As I grasp your hand, I feel a coldness that I have never felt before. This coldness assures me that you are no longer here, it is only your shell that lies here before us.

We are mourning a person whose soul is long gone.
I wonder if you are also hovering over your coffin like a ghost at this moment, watching me. Whether you see all the mourners and are happy that so many people have turned up to say *"Farewell!"* one last time.
I can't bear this sight for long. My eyes fill with tears and my surroundings blur before me.

---

You will never be able to laugh, cry or be happy again. I feel as if you have simply been torn out of life, no, torn out of MY life. Like a plaster that has been ripped off your skin without warning, and the spot now burns like hell.

As if a part of my heart had been taken from me that I hadn't even noticed until the day you died. The wound is bleeding profusely, and this bleeding cannot be stopped. You look so peaceful as you lie there, as if you would wake up at any moment and be able to carry on with your life normally.
But that won't happen. It will never happen again that we laugh, cry or philosophize about life together. Not even on this day in September. There will never be another nice day in September for me without you.

You're gone - John is gone. September was always my favorite month, partly because of you. We celebrated your birthday at the beginning of September, ushering in the best time of the year.
Every September was beautiful with you, every year was beautiful with you. Even when we parted, the memory of your love made me enjoy every September. All that is over now and will never come back.

---

I remember one of your birthdays particularly well. You're wearing a T-shirt from your favorite band. We went to their concerts almost every year back then. I sat on your shoulders, and you gave me your baseball jacket when it got a bit colder outside after the concert.

Today, I'm glad that I still have this jacket - the only thing I have left of yours. It not only reminds me of the many concerts we attended together, it reminds me above all of a carefree time. A time when there was no fear, physical pain or death. Your jacket went well with my hair, because just like the fullness of my hair, the jacket was oversize for me as soon as I wore it. So they complemented each other perfectly.

We didn't talk much about death because we loved life far too much. I think when you're young, life seems like a very long journey - until you realize that it can be just a brief moment when we wake up to capture what we can of life.

In the end, however, we realize that no matter how short or long our life was, we can't hold on to anything in the long run. We only have ourselves on this journey. Just us.

---

By the time we parted, autumn had already moved into our hearts. We were simply too young back then to have survived those four years without emotional damage.
Even after we broke up, I remembered you for a long time. I fondly remember the time when you gave me a quick glance and a reassuring hug to let me know that everything was fine.

Even though these memories often hurt, I was glad to have made them with you. You gave me some of your time and attention as a gift and I knew that I was allowed to be with you as I was.
You accepted me as I was and could hardly take your eyes off me as soon as we met. I felt as if you could not only see my human shell, but also everything that was behind it.
You often said to me back then that beauty fades, but a beautiful character will always shine. I think you were right.

Last night, I looked up at the sky and saw a particularly bright star that I had never noticed before. I think it was your soul lighting up the night sky.

---

Now your eyes have closed forever. You have left this life - our life - forever. Suddenly I feel an uneasy feeling in the region of my heart. This pain quickly brings me back to the present. It feels as if I have swallowed a stone that is now trying to pass through my esophagus but is simply stuck because of its size.

My heart becomes heavy. I just can't manage to swallow the stone. As I didn't know how to say goodbye to you properly, I wrote you a letter. I'm not sure if it contains the right words for what happened between us.
But I wanted to try to share my feelings with you one last time before we never see each other again, and you start your last journey.

I place the letter in front of your coffin, right at the foot, and hope that it will be placed inside as soon as the ceremony is over. At the very end, when you see the light of day for the last time, before you are laid to rest forever.

*Dear John,*

*I am here now. I am very close to you and yet you are so far away. The thought that I will never be able to see you or hear your laughter again tears my heart apart.*

*I haven't thought about you for years, and now all the feelings come flooding back so strongly that I wish we'd had more time together in this world.*

*If only we had laughed together more and spent more time together. We had already spent almost our entire day together, and it still didn't seem like enough to me. Why do memories that took us years to make now feel like seconds?*

*My thoughts fly through the room. You are here and yet you are not. My heart has missed you for the last few years without me knowing it.*

*I want you to know that I will never forget our time together. Standing in front of your grave will be one of the worst moments for me. Your funeral makes everything so finite. So over.*

*I don't know how I'll ever get over this misfortune. How am I supposed to understand that you, the person I loved the most a few years ago, is no longer there?*

*I'll never be able to call you again when I feel like it, I'll never be able to hug you again, and I'll never be able to hear your voice again when we've laughed about something.*

*You will live on in my heart forever. Thank you for the wonderful time I was able to spend with you. You were a great friend. A great man.*
*My one and only.*

*We'll meet again, I'm sure of it. I will recognize you by your smile when we meet in heaven, and by the way you looked at me every time our eyes met.*

*The feeling of familiarity that always surrounded me when you were near me will be my guide.*

*With eternal love,*
*your Josie*

I try not to break down while the mortician delivers your eulogy. It is several pages long and printed on fine, beige-colored tissue paper. It mainly contains key professional information and memories, which the eulogist recalls from your parents' stories.

After the speech, your coffin is lowered into the ground before soil is poured onto it. I just want to leave. I catch sight of your parents again in the mourning crowd. Your mother looks over at me and when she notices that I'm also looking in her direction, she takes a few steps towards me. I don't think I can handle her emotional baggage at this moment, but I don't want to offend her either, so I give her a loving hug.

She's wearing a chic black two-piece suit and has the same blue husky eyes as you. You two look a lot alike and as I hug her, I feel myself hugging a part of you too. That feels good.

Now we're both standing in front of your grave, hand in hand, overwhelmed with our feelings. No one says anything until the ceremony is over. Tears run down my face like streams and I find it difficult to find my bearings.

It's as if it's just me and your mother at this moment. After what feels like an eternity of silence, she turns to me. Her eyes are also swollen, and her face is red from crying.
Her ice-blue eyes are no longer as bright as they were before. They have lost their sparkle. I don't expect either of us to say anything. But to my surprise, your mother speaks up:

*"Josie, I'm so glad you came. John would have loved that, you know? About two weeks ago, he told me that he wanted to call you, but that you had changed your number. I think he wanted to talk to you".*

Your mother's words hit me right in the heart. You wanted to talk to me? I had never received a call. But the fact that you told your mother shows me that it was important to you.

When it came to 'us', you only ever told your parents the bare minimum. I was your treasure and that's why you always wanted to protect me. No one should allow themselves to judge me.

---

Is it really true that you wanted to contact me? Why did you want to talk to me? Apparently you've led a very successful life, why would you want me back in your life?
Were you looking for the security we gave each other when we were young? Did you miss that sense of security? Your new "hip" surroundings are unlikely to have given you that certainty.

Or were you faced with a difficult decision that you didn't want to make alone? I've often read that people who want to start a new chapter in their lives meet up with people from their past - to make sure that their next step really is the right one.
Perhaps you would have wanted to say goodbye to us and our time together and simply left our past life. Just say "Ciao" and then never look back. Close the door and throw away the key forever.

---

I can feel my voice failing. I would like to answer your mother, but I can't. I am too exhausted. My body is exhausted. You were so close to me for a while, we experienced so much, and now I can't tell anyone because YOU are no longer there.

I realize this at this moment. No one will ever know how great you were. I will never be able to introduce you to anyone. Everything that made you was no longer there. YOU were no longer there.

---

Your mother looked at me silently for a while, as if she knew that I had just been lost in my thoughts. She didn't want to disturb me. Maybe you also thought that you were disturbing me with your call and that's why you didn't try to reach me. No matter what the reason was, it had become meaningless with your death.

# 8 Trance

After your funeral, I want to be alone. I'm going to the place we used to call our place. It's high up on a mountain in our town. The highest point with the best view. I loved this place because I was here before I knew you, especially on every beautiful day in September.

Luckily for me, you liked it as much as I did. There is a small field full of sunflowers at the foot of the path, which were also blooming in the most beautiful colors today. Hardly any of the many sunflowers had faded, which was unusual for this time of year. Once I reach the top, I need a moment not to go completely crazy.

Only now do I realize how exhausting the last few days have been, and my body lets me feel it. Thousands of thoughts are racing through my head. My body feels drained, tired and weak. My heart is heavy and I wouldn't be surprised if it stopped working altogether soon.

---

Attending your funeral drained the last of my energy. When your coffin was closed and the cemetery staff carried it to the grave, I could only follow the mourners in disbelief. I just don't understand it.

THIS is supposed to be your end? You're going to be buried in the city where we met and fell in love? I would never have believed that your story would end like this.
The last chapter of your book was written - on a day in September. In moments like these, I wish there was a rewind button or a pause button that would allow me to relive certain situations in life when things weren't going so well.

Simply iron out mistakes that have been made. But time is running out. It's running away from us all and we make mistakes that will shape us for the rest of our lives. Nothing will remain of us once we have left this world. I have lost you. But really, just today? No, I think I lost you the moment we argued for days again.
I lost my love for you in those moments. In the end, I lost you too. We make mistakes every day. Some are not so serious, others are all the more so, and these will affect us for the rest of our lives.

---

I am tormented by inexplicable physical pain. For a moment, I wonder how long a person can survive in such pain. I feel like I'm dying with you, only much slower than you did. This thought makes me feel sick to my stomach. My body is signaling to me that a part of me has actually died.

You are gone. And the part of me that is no longer there leaves a gaping wound in my core. I'm afraid that this wound can't simply be mended. I have suffered a mental injury that cannot simply be repaired, according to the motto: "*A plaster will do!*". I try to breathe in and out deeply, but I quickly fail in this attempt.

---

The ascent was more strenuous for me than ever before. Back then, we conquered this mountain with ease and in no time at all. Now it feels like I'm carrying around a huge ballast that I can't get rid of.
And I haven't really eaten much for days. Nothing is easy anymore. Not this climb, not my life and not my physical condition either. Then I remember why my life seemed so easy back then.

YOU were there and made it easy for me. With you, I felt light, took life easy and was free of any ballast. When I did have burdens to carry, you made it more bearable. The memories of you bring tears to my eyes. They are so tired from crying, and I struggle to keep them open. I can't bear your death. I can't bear the idea that I will never see you again.

I wonder where you are now and whether you remember our time together. Maybe you can't remember us directly, but perhaps you still carry the feeling of our love with you. This thought gives me a little strength. From the highest part of the mountain, I can see our beloved amusement park and imagine that it's not strangers down there, but us teenagers having fun.

Was it a coincidence that we met? Or did fate bring us together back then? It simply can't be a coincidence that we met, of all people. The fact that our paths crossed must have been predetermined. Our journey together must simply have had a purpose. It pains me to think that soon no one will remember you but me.

The memories of you. Of a person who told me back then that rules were only for people without imagination and who bravely stood his ground, no matter how hopeless the situation was.

---

I can see the many children standing at the bottom of the rides. Innocent, carefree and above all happy. *"That was us back then"* I think to myself. These children know nothing of suffering, pain and mental anguish. I soak up the laughter of the little ones as I close my eyes and try to catch my breath one last time before heading back down the mountain.

## 9 Reconsideration

I wake up. A new day has dawned. The day after the worst thing that happened in September. Is it really true that you're not here anymore, John? I try to remember your touch. But neither this memory of you nor your voice can bring me back to the present.

You're gone - it's really true. I stare at the barren ceiling of my bedroom. I cried so much last night that my make-up has smudged and now adorns my pillow.
The imprints of the tears are clearly visible on it, dipped in black paint. The ache in my chest is still firmly in place.
It feels like a part of my youth has been ripped out and with it a part of my human existence. There is now a gaping hole in this part of my body that I can't fill myself.

I miss you so much that I can hardly stand it. I still remember last night's nightmare very well. We met at our fairground as usual. Everything was loud, full of joy and sunshine.

The sun was shining so brightly in your face that your eyes were an even brighter blue than before. You don't say anything. The wind was blowing through our hair and our bellies were full of sweets.

But suddenly night fell. I could no longer see you. The sun went dark and it became quiet. No one was laughing anymore, I couldn't see your shining eyes anywhere and you, the person who had just been standing next to me, had also disappeared.

I couldn't hear any voices, no one was singing with joy, and I was suddenly all alone. Our fairground has become a dreary place, whereas just a moment ago it was full of love and warmth.
The rides stand still. There is no longer a breeze and I feel cold. Everything around me is dark and colorless. It also seems to have become much icier at this moment.
You're gone - again. I wonder if I've lost you and where I can find you so that we can have fun together again - like we did just a moment ago!

A thousand questions are running through my head: where are you and when will you be back?
Then suddenly: a new thought.

You are dead.

New questions.

New thoughts.

What might your last seconds have felt like? What were you thinking? How did you feel? Did you know it was coming to an end? Some people are said to sense their death before it happens, as if they had a sixth sense.

Now I imagine the death scenes from various movies again, in which a person is lying on the ground, obviously injured and close to the end. His spirit hovers above him, still hoping that everything will be alright.

I think it was different for you. Maybe you were scared because you had to lie there all alone on a street in the cold fall. Maybe it happened so quickly that you lost consciousness immediately - no one can say for sure. This uncertainty torments me and I can feel my whole body vibrating with pain, even in my dreams.

The next thing I see is a picture of you. You are smiling. My surroundings change and are bathed in warm light. I feel nothing but peace and harmony.

You are probably now in a place where you are no longer in pain. A place where everything is easy again, just like it was with us back then. No doubts, no fear and no sadness.

Change of scene. From light to dark.

Again, I'm standing alone at the fairground. It's cold again. It's dark again. There is still no one there to help me out. I look down at my feet.

Your old baseball jacket is lying on the grass in front of me. I remember that I kept the jacket in my wardrobe until today, and now I wonder how it got to this place. I pick up the jacket. It smells like you. This scent takes me back to the first day we met, to the library.

Another change. From dark to light.

I'm standing in the library. It's another beautiful day in September. Everything seems to be the same as before. But the library is empty. I don't see you or any other people, and your jacket has suddenly disappeared again. The place seems so peaceful.

I sit down at the table right at the entrance and look out of the window - "*just like before*" I think. Everything seems so calm and harmonious. Nothing here reminds me of what I'm going through right now. No physical pain, no anxiety, just a beautiful day in September.

---

I wake up in a cold sweat and gasp for air. I quickly run to the cupboard where I put your jacket. Phew - it's still there, in the place where I left it. The stone in my chest lightens. I think that by still holding on to your jacket, I can also hold on to the memory of you better. Something that is never lost cannot disappear, can it?

---

I am so exhausted from this dream that I decide to take a long bath, get myself ready and tend to my emotional wounds. Will this nightmare end one day?
Can I ever be happy again without you, John? From one moment to the next, my life turned into a no man's land, from which I will never find my way out on my own.

## 10 Visions of the future

I will always remember the day you died. Why did it have to be a day in September?

I'm sitting on a bench at the entrance to the park and looking up at the sky. The roses are blooming in the most beautiful colors and the whole scene looks very romantic. I haven't been able to visit our fairground for a while. It hurts too much after everything that has happened.
Anger overcomes me.

*"Can you hear me John?"* I whisper softly. A leaf hits my shoulder as I dwell on my thoughts. Even though everything seems so peaceful and beautiful, I'm angry. Angry at you. Why did you just throw your life away like that? Who gave you the right to do that? Do you think nobody cared about you anymore? Or was it just pure stupidity that made you do it? No, you weren't stupid! You could have achieved so much!

I get melancholy because these thoughts haunt me every day. I imagine what would have happened if we hadn't broken up. What would you be like then?

Would you perhaps still be alive? Would we still be happy? I imagine what you would look like today. Tears run down my face.

No, we weren't happy at the end of our relationship. We would probably have destroyed each other - like two stones that keep colliding.

For the last time, I go back to the day I saw you for the first time. My memories flash before my inner eye as if in fast motion. Everything is bright and full of love. You radiate this love. You are also the source of the warmth that comfortably envelops me.

I hear you say again: *"Hey, can you tell me where the philosophy department is?"*. Your eyes shine in such a beautiful husky blue that I am once again speechless and could lose myself in your eyes for hours.

I relive with you all the moments that shaped our relationship. That time was so full of light, warmth and bliss - how could we let our happiness break?

---

I find myself mentally walking through the streets of our city looking for people who are like you. I look for in other people what I found in you. People who are like you were. But I get lost in this search. No matter where I look: I can't find anyone who looks like you.
No one has your eyes, your character or your charm. There is nothing. Nothing to look for and nothing to find. There is no one like you. Nowhere. In no place in this world.

---

A few months after your funeral, I received a letter from your parents. That was surprising for me, as I had never seen or heard from them again since the funeral. I was all the more pleased about what they wanted to tell me.

*Dear Josie,*

*we are so pleased that you were able to attend John's funeral. Everyone had to carry their own burden that day, and burying our son was the biggest challenge of our lives.*

*We hope you can cope with this loss better than we can. After John's death, we broke up his apartment and took back his laptop, some personal belongings, his clothes and his smartphone.*

*We wanted to let you know that we found a lot of photos and videos of you two during the years of your relationship. We thought you would like to have these files back, as they show you and John.*

*We have also sent you other videos and photos showing John in the years after your separation. Maybe you'd like to look at them and see what he's become (without you).*

*We are very proud that he achieved such a good degree and was able to build a great life for himself. Even today, we still talk about him like he's about to walk back in the door, it's crazy.*

*Missing someone and knowing that you will never be able to tell them in person again is destructive. However, with the many files we have found, we now doubt that his life was truly happy and fulfilling.*

*He never spoke much about private matters, but some of his notes show that he often struggled with himself and his new life. We very much hope that you dear Josie are happy with your life. Our only son has left us, please lead a longer, happier life - can you promise us that?*

*Think of these files as a parting gift from John, and remember him as he was to you.*

*Best wishes to you*
*Jane & Walter*

*PS:*
*John's nursery is still as it was when he was young. When he moved away to start his Master's degree, we didn't change anything until today.*

*Maybe you would like to come over and pick out some mementos? John always seemed to like you very much and never forgot you.*
*All the best until then.*

After reading this letter, I had to sit down for a moment. John, there you were again. Our connection had not been severed. I was so glad that you hadn't forgotten me. I drove to your parents' house, where they were already waiting for me with tears in their eyes.
We hugged each other long and hard, even though we had never done this before - except at your funeral. I felt as if everything was meant to be just like that at this moment.

I was wearing your old baseball jacket and your parents seemed visibly moved by the gesture. I felt a sense of togetherness, a feeling that I had only felt with you until that day.
As if you had brought us together or reunited us. I suddenly felt as close to you again as if you had just been here. Maybe that's what you were. In any case, it felt good and right to be here.

When I opened the door to your room, I was met by a familiar smell. The smell of your perfume. I imagined that you had just been here a moment ago and had just left to get something. The whole room is filled with your aura and the love you have shown me.

You are gone. I just can't believe it. The world stands still and someone has just stopped time in your room.

## 11. Our heaven

I had closed the door to your room, and now there was nothing but silence in here. When I closed the door, I entered another world - your world. The world that was also mine in my youth.
I sat here in your baseball jacket and let my eyes wander around the room. It was one of those beautiful, warm days in September. The sun was shining through the nursery window, making the room feel bright and peaceful. I felt really safe when I dropped onto your bed.

The bed was exactly the same as it had been back then. Your parents really hadn't changed anything since you left. On the edge of the bed I found our old 'markers', as we used to call them. By markings, I mean initials and words that we had carved into it back then.

As your bed was a wooden bed, we immortalized the titles and page numbers of our favorite books in many places. You told me back then that you could fall asleep better if you remembered all the stories we had read together.
My gaze wanders to a special marker: "*J.J. - p. 16 paragraph 8*" is written there, almost neatly, engraved into the wood.

The Australian author Jen Johnson - known for her tragic love stories - particularly appealed to us at the time. Although her books often ran to well over 500 pages, we read every one of her works as if we were addicted to them. When I saw the marker, I wondered what Jen Johnson would write about us. Would our sad love story have been enough material for one of her books?

Our great urge to read enabled us to finish one of her books within two days. Afterwards, we could philosophize for hours about the book's subject. Especially when you started your studies, this approach was perfect because you had to read a lot and I benefited from the new literature.
This author was unique because she described tragic and dramatic events in relationships - but she did so sensitively, as only she could.

The marker pointed to a chapter in her book "The Invisible Stranger". This work had particularly fascinated us because it was about a woman who had lost her husband in an accident. Despite this, she believed that she kept receiving signs from him from the afterlife.
Even then, John and I firmly believed that there had to be something like an energy from the afterlife. I still remember the following passage that we engraved on John's bed.

*"And so you stood before me. I couldn't see you, I couldn't touch you - only feel you. It was you who told me in this way that you had not forgotten me.*

*Your radiant presence broke through the boundaries of the two worlds. We were united in a way that transcended all rational boundaries.*

*I looked at you and then again I didn't. I felt you, and then again I didn't. You were here - and then again not."*

---

We discussed for hours whether this was really the spirit of her husband, or perhaps the energy of God that the woman perceived. At the end of the book, this woman met a man who had very similar behavior and thinking to her deceased husband.

So it was as if her husband had been reincarnated into another person - crazy, right? Again, I thought of the last sentence of this section: *"I felt you, and then again I didn't, you were here and then again you weren't"*.
It reminded me so much of my current situation. I felt an inner urge to find the book with you right now. I wanted to touch it, as if I could touch you through it.

Just for a brief moment, I wanted to feel you, touch you, experience you and bring back the memory. It had to be somewhere on your bookshelf. I went in search of it. With over 500 books that you had bought over the years, this was no easy task.

In addition, many of your books were very dusty, which is why I suffered a spontaneous coughing fit - which forced me to open the window first, even though I was afraid that your scent would evaporate, and I would no longer be able to catch it. Something that is never lost cannot disappear, can it?

After a while, I tracked down the work in question. It was at the top of the bookshelf and was more than a little dusty. I took it off the shelf and held it as if touching the book would bring back all the past moments.

My mind went crazy. I saw us cowering in front of your bed as teenagers, laughing and carving our initials into the bed. You look at me, I look at you. All is right with the world. Our world is fine.

I quickly search for the section to check whether I was remembering the passage that had fascinated us both so much. I opened the first page of the book and three photos suddenly fell out of the flap. Pictures that showed us. I carefully placed the book and the pictures on your bed.

It had a wonderful cover because it showed two people as spirits dancing together in the universe - detached from time and space, as if there were no limits to love.
Everything was very delicately designed and underlaid with mystical, dark colors. The two "spirit souls", as I call them, could not be united on earth. But in the universe they found a place where this was possible.

So not even death could separate their love and affection for each other. At the time, I found this story very romantic. Now that I've been in a similar situation myself, I can only empathize with the pain the main character of this story had to suffer.

---

The photos show us in happy years. How we laugh and have fun with our lives. We are fooling around and seem happy to have each other.
One picture shows the little field of sunflowers in full bloom. Another shows us standing in the middle of the field and beaming with the yellow flowers.

In all the pictures, you're wearing your baseball jacket, and I'm wearing my curly, voluminous hair loose, which unfortunately obscures most of the surroundings and now nothing can be seen in the background. However, this doesn't detract from our radiance.

We look content. When and why did this feeling change? When did we become the people we are today? Today. Once again, I find myself talking about you in the present instead of the past.
As if you had never left. As if you were still here. The state of your room shows me that time must have stood still here. You're only gone for a moment and I'm waiting for you on your bed. I read. I breathe. I wait.

---

I could see every part of the room from the bed. This reminded me of the good times. We used to read for hours in that room. It was everyone for himself - you in a corner of the room, me on your bed - so that after our reading time we could tell each other about the latest discoveries and stories.
We spent so many hours in that room laughing, rejoicing and sometimes crying. It's unbelievable how quickly time has passed, and we've grown up.

I feel as if I'm living in this exact time and have only grown older. Life has simply gone on without me. I may have grown up and literally outgrown our experiences, but I'm still stuck in a world in between. When I realize this, I suddenly realize that I can no longer live in our world - the past.

All the pictures on your wardrobe, all the moments and memories lived, are in the past. YOU are the past. Those people no longer exist, just like those moments.

---

When we are young, we have a different image of the people around us and our sphere of life. Years later, this image can change because our perceptions are constantly changing and life shapes us. John was always my hero. I don't think there was anyone I admired more at the time.

But I couldn't admire the person John became. I didn't want to believe that he had voluntarily chosen this direction, but he did. My illusion about him was shattered on September 16. Had my perception deceived me like that? Had John not been the person I thought he was? Or did he just meet the wrong friends who influenced him in a bad way?

I will probably never understand John's path in life, and now was the time to put all this behind me and look ahead. To a new future. Without John.

## 12. Tomorrow

I visited John's home one last time years later. It was the day his parents decided to sell their house - because they had become too old to look after it. I wanted to say goodbye to the home that had also been my home for a while.

I entered the narrow hallway and climbed the stairs to his room. The old staircase still made the same noises as when we used to run around the house as teenagers. So not much had changed on the outside. It was only inside that everything had changed.

The rooms in the house were still full of memories. There was a part of our past in every fiber of the wallpaper and in every piece of the floor. A kind of imprint; something that made this house what it was and breathed life into it. Seeing the now empty rooms made me wistful.

That pain rose up in my chest again, feeling as heavy as a stone. Until that moment, I thought I had long since overcome John's loss, but I was far from it. I saw John's parents for the last time that day, even though I didn't realize it at the time.

---

A few years later, I read in the newspaper that an elderly couple had died in a car accident. It was your parents, John, who lost their lives on a highway on an autumnal September day. The accident happened on your day, September 16th.

A wrong-way driver had lost control on a wet road and crashed into their car - they didn't stand a chance. I know that your parents loved you very much and were never able to come to terms with your loss - the death of their only son - for the rest of their lives.

Now you are hopefully reunited in peace and can find your final rest together. As I reflect on this misfortune, I realize how short our lives are. One moment we are here, laughing, living. The next moment, it's all over. Our life is over.
No one knows when it will be, we can only hope that we all have a few days left to love, to breathe, to live.

---

For my part, I lived for quite a while with the thought of what would have become of John and me if we hadn't split up back then.

Living in a world where he no longer existed was incredibly difficult for me. I was lucky enough to be able to stay in this world for over sixty years after his death and to experience many sunrises and sunsets.

---

Many years after John's death, I met a handsome, smart man named Jeff. He was thoughtful, loving and very creative. I fell in love with him immediately and we started a relationship. We bought a house and lived happily together until his death. We had never spent a second of our lives apart. When he fell ill with cancer at the age of 70, I was by his side until his last breath.

When we bought our house, it was in great need of renovation. I took care of the interior and exterior decorating, while Jeff did most of the handyman work. Whenever I watched Jeff at work, I noticed how similar John and Jeff actually were. Jeff was tall, dark-haired and his eyes were a similar cool color to John's, just not quite as bright.

When we're young, we have a different image of love. We strive for perfection. As we get older, our idea gradually shifts and this image changes. Jeff was my hero until the end. I don't think there is anyone I admire more at this time.

---

I am now 86 years old myself and will probably pass away from this world in the foreseeable future. I can feel this feeling spreading more and more inside me that it will soon be time to say goodbye. I hope I will see you both, Jeff and John, again in heaven.
Don't hold it against me, Jeff, if I still think about John a lot now. I have really tried to turn over a new leaf. But love that you once experienced at a young age often stays in your heart forever.

Since I am also very grateful to you, Jeff, for the wonderful time here on earth, I wanted to leave no stone unturned in expressing my deep love to you as well.

I did this by writing you a letter, which I put in an envelope and placed at your gravestone. It contained the following lines.

*Dear Jeff,*

*thank you for everything you have done for me. You were always a loving husband, and I hope that you are now in a place where you no longer have to endure pain.*

*You fulfilled many of my wishes, and with you, I was able to fly high without ever having to fall low. You were and are my treasure, the man who enriched my life with so much sunshine that others would simply be dazzled.*

*Our time together was wonderful, and I can count myself lucky that I was able to spend my life with someone like you.*

*I will love you forever.*
*Your Josie*

Do you also know those people who come into our lives and whose peculiarities you will never forget? The way someone wears their hair, a distinctive eye color or the sound of their voice when they laugh? Details that we will never forget. These memories stay in our hearts and in our minds forever.

John had this special quality. I would still recognize his eyes 50 years from now among thousands of people because they were so unique. That look that seemed so familiar and mysterious to me every time we met. I would probably never have enough of him. Only John could touch my heart like that. I would have loved to sink into his eyes when we met and just look at him for hours. I guess I could never really fully comprehend his beauty.

---

I visited John's grave one last time. The walk was difficult, my bones ached on this summer day, and I knew I had to memorize his grave site forever. I would probably never be able to return to this place again - at least not alive.

The sun was shining brightly from the sky that day; it had turned out to be a beautiful day in September. Life had been kind to me, and I remembered all the beautiful days we had spent together in September.

I laid down a bouquet of sunflowers, whose color shone like John's eyes back then. But it was nowhere near as beautiful as the bouquet of sunflowers John had always given me.
But today, I didn't just bring John flowers. I opened my box of memories one last time, which also contained John's old baseball jacket. I've been saving it for this long, but now I think it's time to give it back to him.

I think by still holding on to his jacket, I could also hold on to the memory of him. Something that is never lost can never disappear, can it?

After all these years, however, I had to realize that it wasn't the old baseball jacket that reminded me of John, because I hadn't opened the box in years. No, it was the memories in my heart that kept him alive for me. It was time to let go of the jacket and let the memories of him rest.

It looked as if the headstone had only just been put up, although the funeral had been several decades ago. It was very important to his parents at the time that he received an appropriate stone, which is why I think John's gravestone is particularly beautiful.
It shines snow-white and has fine, dark brown, marbled lines running through it. It resembles a real rock in the sea that nothing can shake.

When the sunlight shines on it, the surface glistens like snow on an icy winter morning. John's face is engraved in the center of the gravestone. He is smiling. The photo shows him when he was younger. It was taken by me on graduation day, the day he was so proud of his certificate.

I wondered what John would be like today, what kind of person he would have become if this accident hadn't happened. How icy blue would his eyes still be today?
But that sparkle had gone out the day John left our world.

As I looked at the graves to the left and right of John, which now belonged to his parents, I was overcome by a queasy feeling. I sensed that I would soon be following John.
I placed my jacket neatly next to his grave. The young John from the photo smiled at me, and I smiled back one last time. But this smile wasn't just a mimic gesture, it was my way of saying *"Farewell!"* to John.

---

We didn't talk much about death, because we loved life far too much. I think when you're young, life seems like a very long journey - until you realize that it can also be just a brief moment when we wake up to capture what we can of life.

In the end, however, we realize that no matter how short or long our life was, we can't hold on to anything in the long run. We only have ourselves on this journey. Just us.

---

True love never dies. We cannot suppress or deny the feelings. They are present and will accompany us throughout our lives. They are the moments of happiness that warm us when it's not a beautiful day outside in September. They accompany us, and we carry the memories of them in our innermost being. With every minute, every breath and every second of our lives.

*Do you also know these people who enter our lives and whose characteristics you will never forget?*

# Epilogue

Josie fell asleep peacefully at the age of 86 in the house she had so lovingly prepared with Jeff. At the moment of her passing, Josie knew that she had made it - the moment had come.

She felt at peace with herself and the people who had crossed her path. Josie was now ready to leave this world. She sat on the corner of her bed one last time to catch the rays of sunlight that had just shone through her porch window.

In the months after Jeff's death, she had sorted through photos and other mementos from the past and stacked them neatly on the dining table. Now there was nothing left but Josie's memories of days gone by. Memories of people who had gone before her. Now it was her turn. It was the beginning of a new month. It was the beginning of September. It was John's birthday.

*"So this is how it ends"* Josie thought to herself as a tear ran down her face. Her body stopped aging, her once powerful heart slowed down, the energy drained from every cell in her body.

Her last breath was for the person she had never forgotten and who had shaped her life in so many ways. With the last of her strength, she whispered "*John*" one last time, as if to give him a signal, a sign that she was now ready for her final journey.

A journey that John had embarked on so many years ago. Without Josie. Without saying goodbye. Not knowing when they would see each other again. Josie's body went limp, her spirit slipping away from her body. She died alone but content and set off on her final journey.

A few days later, she was buried next to her husband in the municipal cemetery. Their graves are only a few meters away from John's grave. A lot of people came to Josie's funeral, and they miss her dearly.

---

Suddenly - silence. Josie feels light, almost weightless. She feels as if a foreign force has gained power over her body. She does not resist. The invisible force carries her almost naturally to a certain place.

Josie can't believe it when she sees the old high school hall in front of her, where she celebrated his graduation with John.

She pauses for a moment. She remembers how beautifully decorated the room was and the overwhelming feeling of happiness she felt when she danced with John. They were both happy. Carefree. Free.

But this is not the hall from back then. It couldn't possibly be, because Josie was old - and this hall clearly wasn't. Josie is no longer the young girl she was back then - or is she? She begins to doubt herself, because when she looks down at herself, her skin is no longer saggy or even wrinkled.
She is back in her youthful body, wearing the long, tight-fitting red dress with a slit, which accentuates her skin and hair color particularly well, and can even smell the scent of her favorite perfume.

She looks around the room. But no matter how hard she tries, there is nothing here that reminds her of the past. Although the room has a similar design to the old days, the glittering disco balls on the ceiling and the music that filled the room are missing and as Josie takes a closer look at the situation, she realizes that the room is also deserted.

It seems as if a lot of things had been decorated for a party that never took place. The end of the room is nowhere to be seen. The further Josie goes into the room, the darker it gets.

But stop.

Suddenly, Josie sees a light shining at the end of the room. It shines so brightly that it suddenly lights up the whole room. Josie approaches the light, albeit somewhat skeptically, and walks towards it.
The light seems to be some kind of energy that wants to cast a spell over Josie. She gets closer and closer to the light, so that her red dress now glitters like a thousand stars in the firmament. The cone of light is so magical that for a moment she has to look at her glittering dress herself and marvel in fascination at the light patterns that are reflected on the walls throughout the room. The energy shines brighter and brighter and gets warmer the closer Josie gets to it.

---

Friends, relatives and members of Jeff's family came to pay their last respects to Josie. Even John's sister, who was now the same age as Josie, attended the funeral.

But it wasn't just human souls who were at Josie's grave site at the time. It seemed as if a familiar energy, an invisible force, had appeared and was silently taking part in Josie's funeral.

This power flowed through the grass of the cemetery, settled in the blossoms of magnificent-looking flowers, and could also be perceived in the air by particularly sensitive people. Josie's coffin was laid out. She looked like an angel. Her dark, curly hair had turned white, but had lost none of its charm and fullness.

The unknown energy hovered over her coffin and only disappeared when it was lowered to the ground and Josie was laid to rest.

This is how Josie's story comes to an end. All the emotions, the love, the sadness that existed some time ago and which determined Josie's life, now rested with her in this peaceful place.

---

Suddenly the energy goes out. It goes dark around Josie for a moment. A muted cone of light now forms around her

dress. Then a person emerges from the darkness. Josie can only recognize this by the sound the soles of their shoes make on the parquet floor.
She feels transported back to the time of the prom.
"*You're here!*" comes from the darkness. Josie recognizes the voice immediately, but still can't believe it.

Slowly, the unknown person steps further and further out of the darkness into the light. The pitch-black hair carefully framing the face, the husky blue eyes and the endearing tone of the voice leave no doubt - it's John!

"*... even the most beautiful flower fades after a while. But in me, our garden of love will flourish forever.*"

*True love never dies. It accompanies us and we carry the memory of it in our innermost being. With every minute, every breath and every second of our lives.*

*Do you also know these people who enter our lives and whose special qualities you will never forget?*

*"I looked at you and then again I didn't. I felt you, and then again I didn't, you were here - and then again, you weren't."*

Author Julia Bittner has published her first romance novel, "A Beautiful Day in September". She has had a penchant for tragic stories and events since her youth, which is why it is no surprise that this debut work about two lovers who have lost sight of each other but never lost heart was penned by her.

Growing up in Chemnitz, Saxony she has embraced the genre of drama, and decided to write a novel about her favorite month, September. She wants to take readers to a place where it is irrelevant whether the protagonists are in the afterlife or the present, and has written a novel that addresses the emotional world of the individual on various levels.

# Novels in English

A beautiful day
in September

978-3-911030-51-9

The tragedy of life
3 short stories

978-3-911030-53-3

**69 DAYS OF SIN**
**MALE EDITION**
978-3-911030-74-8

**69 DAYS OF SIN**
**FEMALE EDITION**
978-3-911030-75-5

**69 DAYS OF SIN**
**COUPLE EDITION**
978-3-911030-76-2

# Guidebooks in English

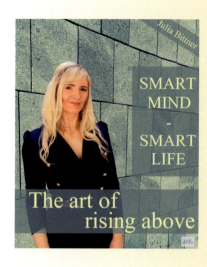

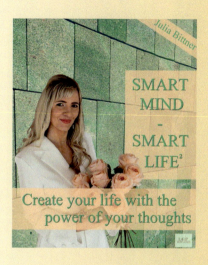

**SMART MIND SMART LIFE**

The art of rising above

978-3-911030-95-3

**SMART MIND SMART LIFE²**

Create your life with the power of your thoughts

978-3-911030-94-6

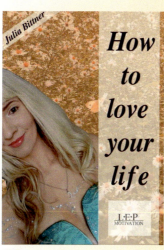

**How to love your life**
**978-3-911030-47-2**

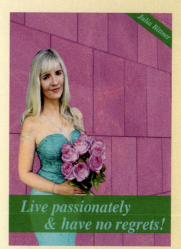

Live passionately
& have no regrets!
978-3-911030-49-6

The six levels of life
978-3-911030-30-4

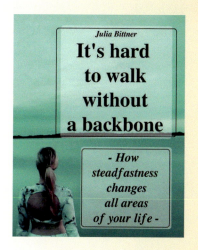
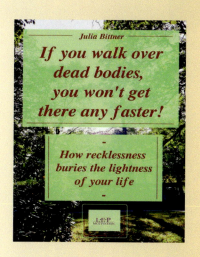

It's hard to walk
without a backbone

978-3-911030-57-1

If you walk over dead
bodies, you won't get
there any faster!
978-3-911030-59-5

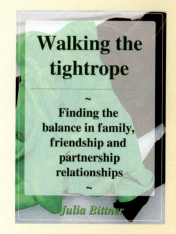

Walking the Tightrope
978-3-911030-55-7

# Discover the LEP ARTBOOKS!

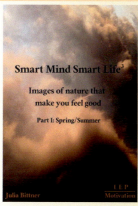 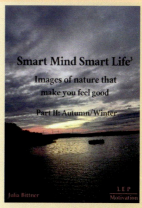

SMART MIND SMART LIFE[3]
Images of nature that make you feel good
*Part I: Spring/Summer*
978-3-911030-38-0

SMART MIND SMART LIFE[3]
Images of nature that make you feel good
*Part II: Autumn/Winter*
978-3-911030-11-3

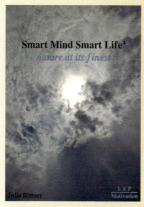

SMART MIND SMART LIFE[4]
*~ nature at its finest ~*
978-3-911030-13-7

SMART MIND SMART LIFE[6]
~ head in the clouds ~
978-3-911030-21-2

SMART MIND SMART LIFE[5]
~ the life of plants trough
colorless glasses ~
978-3-911030-15-1

SMART MIND SMART LIFE[7]
~ undiscovered beauty ~
978-3-911030-23-6

SMART MIND SMART LIFE[8]
Always look on the
nature side of life
978-3-911030-98-4

## Lyrical desserts for the soul - FOR FREE!

### The 69 DAYS EXPERIENCE - Poems

### Success Guide - LEP-Motivation

## Astrology is the key - Guide

## A beautiful day in September
## - Visions -

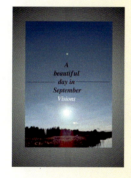

## *Coming soon*

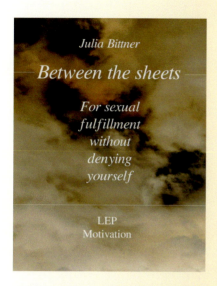

**Between the sheets**

~

**For sexual fulfillment without denying yourself**

~

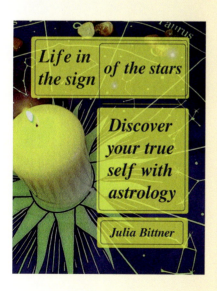

**Life in the sign of the stars**

~

**Discover your true self with astrology**

~

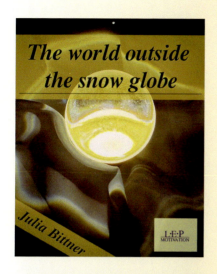

*The world outside the snowglobe*

*~ Guidebook ~*

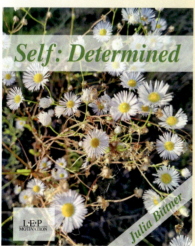

*Self : Determined*

*Self : Confident*

*~ Guidebook ~*

## LEP-MOTIVATION

- Mental coaching
- Astrological counseling
- Spiritual counseling (Tarot)
- Psychological counseling
- Conflict resolution
- Guided meditation
- Individual & couples counseling
  Focus: Relationships and sexuality

+ 49 (0) 178 869 1500 // info@lep-motivation.com
www.lep-motivation.com

**Visit our
store on Etsy!**

www.etsy.com/shop/
katthemythswireland

---

**Scan the code and start
reading NOW!**

 **Instagram**:
lepmotivation

**Questions and ideas:**
info@lep-motivation.com

 **LEP-Motivation**
Postfach (P.O. Box) 71 01 02
09056 Chemnitz

-Germany-

# L·E·P
## LIFE EMOTION PLAN

**For more information, please visit:**

www.lep-motivation.com